THE AMELIA BEDELIA TREASURY

GOOD WORK, AMELIA BEDELIA
AMELIA BEDELIA AND THE BABY
AMELIA BEDELIA HELPS OUT

by **Peggy Parish**
pictures by **Lynn Sweat**

SCHOLASTIC INC.
New York Toronto London Auckland Sydney
Mexico City New Delhi Hong Kong

ISBN 0-590-98470-5

Good Work, Amelia Bedelia
Text copyright © 1976 by Margaret Parish.
Illustrations copyright © 1976 by Lynn Sweat.

Amelia Bedelia and the Baby
Text copyright © 1981 by Margaret Parish.
Illustrations copyright © 1981 by Lynn Sweat.

Amelia Bedelia Helps Out
Text copyright © 1979 by Margaret Parish.
Illustrations copyright © 1979 by Lynn Sweat.

12 11 10 9 8 7 6 5   2 3/0

Printed in the U.S.A.   23

First Scholastic printing, November 1998

GOOD WORK, AMELIA BEDELIA

by Peggy Parish

pictures by Lynn Sweat

For Sam and David Rogers

with love

GOOD WORK, AMELIA BEDELIA

"Amelia Bedelia," called Mr. Rogers.

"Is the coffee ready?"

"Coming right up," said Amelia Bedelia.

She poured a cup of coffee.

She took it into the dining room.

"There," said Amelia Bedelia.

"Would you like something more?"

"Yes," said Mr. Rogers.

"Toast and an egg."

"Fine," said Amelia Bedelia.

She went into the kitchen.

Very quickly

Amelia Bedelia was back.

Mr. Rogers picked up the egg.

He broke it over his toast.

"Confound it, Amelia Bedelia!"

he said. "I didn't say raw egg!"

"But you didn't say to cook it,"

said Amelia Bedelia.

Mr. Rogers threw down his napkin.

"Oh, go fly a kite," he said.

Amelia Bedelia looked surprised.

"All right," she said. "If you say so."

Soon Amelia Bedelia was out in a field.

She had a kite.

"Now that was nice of Mr. Rogers,"

she said. "I do love to fly kites.

But I better get back.

Mrs. Rogers might need me."

Sure enough, Mrs. Rogers was calling,

"Amelia Bedelia."

"Here I am," said Amelia Bedelia.

"There's a lot to do,"

said Mrs. Rogers.

"Do you know how to make bread?"

"I make good corn bread,"

said Amelia Bedelia.

"No, I want white bread,"

said Mrs. Rogers.

"You are a good cook.

Just do what the recipe says."

"All right," said Amelia Bedelia.

"Here's a list of the other things
I want you to do," said Mrs. Rogers.
"I'll be out until dinner time."
"Don't worry," said Amelia Bedelia.
"I'll get everything done."
Mrs. Rogers left.

"I'll start with that bread,"
said Amelia Bedelia.
She read the recipe.
"Do tell," she said.
"I never knew
bread did magic things."

Amelia Bedelia got everything
she needed.
Quickly she mixed the dough.

Amelia Bedelia

set the pan on the table.

"Now," she said,

"you're supposed to rise.

This I've got to see."

Amelia Bedelia sat down to watch.

But nothing happened.

"Maybe you don't like to be watched.

I'll come back," said Amelia Bedelia.

"Let's see."

Amelia Bedelia got her list.

"Clean out the ashes

in the parlor fireplace.

Fill the wood box."

Amelia Bedelia went into the parlor.

She cleaned out the ashes.

And Amelia Bedelia filled

the wood box.

"That's done," said Amelia Bedelia.

"What's next?"

She read, "Pot the window box plants.

Put the pots in the parlor."

Amelia Bedelia went outside.

She counted the plants.

Then she went into the kitchen.

"My goodness," she said.

"I need every pot for this."

So she took them all.

Amelia Bedelia potted those plants.

And she took them inside.

"Now I better tend to that bread,"
said Amelia Bedelia.
She went into the kitchen.
But the bread still sat on the table.
"Now look here," she said.
"You are supposed to rise.
Then I'm supposed to punch you down.
How can I punch if you don't rise?"
Amelia Bedelia sat down to think.
"Maybe that pan is too heavy,"
she said.
"I better help it rise."

Amelia Bedelia got some string.

She worked for a bit.

And that bread began to rise.

"That should be high enough,"

said Amelia Bedelia.

"I'll just let you stay there awhile."

Amelia Bedelia picked up her list.

"'Make a sponge cake.'"

Amelia Bedelia read that again.

"I know about a lot of cakes,"

she said.

"And I never heard tell of that.

But if she wants a sponge cake,

I'll make her a sponge cake."

Amelia Bedelia put a little of this
and some of that into a bowl.
She mixed and mixed.
"Now for that sponge," she said.
Amelia Bedelia got a sponge.
She snipped it into small pieces.
"There," she said.
"Into the cake you go."

Soon the sponge cake was baking.

"I don't think Mr. Rogers

will like this cake,"

said Amelia Bedelia.

"I'll make my kind of cake too.

He does love butterscotch icing."

So Amelia Bedelia

baked another cake.

"There now," she said.

"I'll surprise him."

Amelia Bedelia put

the butterscotch cake in the cupboard.

She put the sponge cake on a shelf.

"My, this is a busy day,"
said Amelia Bedelia.
"Let's see what's next.
'Call Alcolu. Ask him to patch
the front door screen.'"
Amelia Bedelia shook her head.
"Alcolu can't patch anything,"
she said. "I better do that myself."
She got what she needed.

And Amelia Bedelia patched that screen.

Amelia Bedelia looked at the time.

"Oh," she said.

"I better get dinner started.

Let me see what she wants."

She read the list.

"'A chicken dinner will be fine.'"

Amelia Bedelia shook her head.

"What will she think of next?" she said.

"Well, that won't take long to fix."

Amelia Bedelia got everything ready.

She set the table.

Then she sat down to rest.

Soon Mr. and Mrs. Rogers came home.

"Amelia Bedelia," yelled Mr. Rogers.

"Coming," called Amelia Bedelia.

"What is that awful cloth
on the front door?" said Mrs. Rogers.

"You said to patch the screen,"
said Amelia Bedelia.
"Can't patch without a patch."

They went into the parlor.

"All my good pots!" said Mrs. Rogers.

"And bad ones too,"

said Amelia Bedelia.

Mr. Rogers looked at the wood box.

He shook his head.

But he didn't say a word.

They went into the kitchen.

"The sponge cake is pretty,"

said Mrs. Rogers.

"At least that's done right."

Something caught Mr. Rogers's eye.

He looked up.

"What in tarnation is that?" he said.

"The bread!" said Amelia Bedelia.

"I plumb forgot it.

Do let me punch it down quick."

She climbed up on a chair.

Amelia Bedelia began to punch.

Mr. and Mrs. Rogers just stared.

The bread plopped to the floor.

"Did I see what I thought I saw?"
said Mr. Rogers.

"You did," said Mrs. Rogers.

"Now," said Amelia Bedelia,

"dinner is ready when you are."

"Well, you can cook," said Mrs. Rogers.

"Dinner should be good."

"I hope so," said Mr. Rogers.

"I'm hungry."

"Just serve the plates,"

said Mrs. Rogers.

Mr. and Mrs Rogers sat at the table.

Amelia Bedelia brought in the plates.

Mr. and Mrs. Rogers stared at the plates.

"But, but, that's cracked corn.

It's all kinds of awful things,"

said Mrs. Rogers.

"You said chicken dinner,"

said Amelia Bedelia.

"That's what chickens eat for dinner."

Mrs. Rogers was too angry to speak.

"Take this mess away,"

said Mr. Rogers.

Mrs. Rogers said,

"Serve the cake and coffee."

Amelia Bedelia did.

Mr. Rogers took a big bite of cake.

He spluttered and spit it out.

"What in tarnation is in that?" he said.

"Sponge," said Amelia Bedelia.

"Mrs. Rogers said

to make a sponge cake."

Suddenly Mr. Rogers laughed.

He roared.

Mrs. Rogers looked at the lumpy cake.

Then she laughed too.

"But I'm still hungry,"

said Mr. Rogers.

"I can fix that," said Amelia Bedelia.

"I have a surprise for you."

"Oh no!" said Mr. Rogers.

"I can't stand another one,"

said Mrs. Rogers.

Amelia Bedelia brought in milk

and her butterscotch cake.

"Ahh," said Mr. Rogers.

"Hurry," said Mrs. Rogers.

"Give me some."

Soon the whole cake was gone.

"How do you do it, Amelia Bedelia?"
said Mr. Rogers. "One minute
we're hopping mad at you."
"And the next, we know we can't
do without you," said Mrs. Rogers.

Amelia Bedelia smiled.

"I guess I just understand your ways,"
she said.

AMELIA BEDELIA AND THE BABY

by PEGGY PARISH

Pictures by Lynn Sweat

AMELIA BEDELIA AND THE BABY

For Jennifer and Jay Thompson,

with love

—P.P.

For Peggy

—L.S.

"But Mrs. Rogers,"
said Amelia Bedelia.
"I don't know a thing
about babies.
How can I babysit?"
"Why, Amelia Bedelia!"
said Mrs. Rogers.
"You are very good
with children."
"Yes," said Amelia Bedelia.
"I get along fine
with children."

"Babies are children, too,"
said Mrs. Rogers.
"If you say so,"
said Amelia Bedelia.
"Now you run along,"
said Mrs. Rogers.
"Mrs. Lane is waiting."

So Amelia Bedelia ran
to Mrs. Lane's house.

She knocked on the door.

"Do come in," said Mrs. Lane.

"I'm already late.

Here is your list.
I hope I didn't forget anything.
But you will know what to do."
"I will?" said Amelia Bedelia.

"I gave Missy her lunch,"
said Mrs. Lane.
"She is in her playpen."
Mrs. Lane left.
"How about that?"
said Amelia Bedelia.
"Babies are kept in pens."
Amelia Bedelia found Missy.
"Hi, Missy," she said.

Missy looked at Amelia Bedelia.
She began to cry.
"Oh, oh," said Amelia Bedelia.
"What should I do?
What does the list say?"

Amelia Bedelia read,
"Give Missy a bottle."

She hurried to the kitchen.
Then she stopped.
"That can't be right,"
said Amelia Bedelia.
"Babies shouldn't have bottles.
They could break."

She thought a bit.
"I know," she said.
"I'll give her a can
or maybe a box."

Missy howled louder.
"I'll give her both,"
said Amelia Bedelia.
And she did.

Missy picked up the can.
She threw it.
She picked up the box.
She threw it.
And she howled.

"All right," said Amelia Bedelia.
"I'll find something else."
She gave Missy one thing
after another.
But Missy just howled louder.

"Maybe you are hungry,"
said Amelia Bedelia.
"I'll get you a cookie."
She ran to the kitchen.
The back door opened.
"Anybody home?"
called Mrs. Carter.

"I'm here," said Amelia Bedelia.

"Here are some strawberries," said Mrs. Carter.

"I hear Missy.
Why is she crying?"

"Beats me," said Amelia Bedelia.
"I'm at my wit's end."

"Have you given her a bottle?" said Mrs. Carter.

"A bottle!" said Amelia Bedelia.
"I have not."

"I think that is what
she wants," said Mrs. Carter.
"I will fix one for her.
You put the strawberries
in something else.
I need my basket."
"All right," said Amelia Bedelia.

Soon Mrs. Carter said,
"The bottle is ready."
"Good," said Amelia Bedelia.
"Here is your basket."
Mrs. Carter left.

Amelia Bedelia looked at the bottle.
"Always something new," she said.
"This bottle won't break.
It's just fine for babies."

She gave the bottle
to Missy.
Missy stopped crying.
"I am glad to know about
those bottles," said Amelia Bedelia.
"They do shush up babies."

Missy finished her bottle.
Amelia Bedelia looked at the list.
"Good," she said.
"You get a bath now.
I know about that."
Amelia Bedelia got
everything ready.
She put Missy in the tub.

Soon Missy was all clean.

"That's done," said Amelia Bedelia.

"Back into your pen you go."

Amelia Bedelia got the list.

She read, "Be sure

to use the baby powder."

She found the powder.

And Amelia Bedelia used it.

"My, I smell good," she said.
"That was nice of Mrs. Lane.
Now what does she want me to do?"
She looked at the list.

"From two until three
is naptime," said Amelia Bedelia.
She shook her head.
"No!" said Amelia Bedelia.
"I won't do it.
I won't take a nap. I hate naps!"

Amelia Bedelia thought a bit.
Then she said, "I know!
Those strawberries!
I will make a surprise.
I do make good strawberry tarts."

She started for the kitchen.
"First," she said,
"I'll see what Missy is doing."
She went to the playpen.

"How about that!
Missy likes naps,"
said Amelia Bedelia.
"She can take mine for me.
I've got better things to do."

She went to the kitchen.
She put some of this
and a little of that
into a bowl.

She mixed and mixed.
Soon her tarts were made.
"Those do look pretty,"
she said.

She put the tarts away.
Missy began to cry.
"Missy is awake,"
said Amelia Bedelia.
"Let me see what
I should do."

"It says to give her
a mashed banana," she said.
"That will be easy."
She got a banana.
And she mashed it.
"This is fun," said Amelia Bedelia.
"But I better give it to Missy."

Missy took the banana.
She looked at it.
Then she mashed it.

She mashed it harder and harder.
Suddenly the skin popped.
Banana squished all over Missy.

Missy clapped her hands.
Then she ate the squishy banana.
Amelia Bedelia laughed.
"I never saw anything like
that before," she said.
"But she had fun.
And it was her banana."

Then Missy began to fuss.
"I can forget the list for now,"
said Amelia Bedelia.
"I know what you need.
You need another bath."

So Missy got another bath.
"Babies do need a lot of washing,"
said Amelia Bedelia.
She dressed Missy.
"Now back to the list," she said.

"Put Missy
in her stroller,"
she read.
Amelia Bedelia
did that.
Then she read,
"But first, put a sweater on her."

Amelia Bedelia
took Missy
out of the stroller.
"Your mama should
have said that first,"
said Amelia Bedelia.

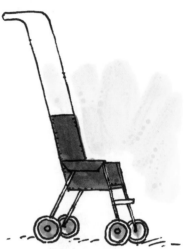

She put a sweater on Missy.
"Back in you go," she said.

She looked at the list again.
"Tarnation!" she said.
"Your mama can't make
up her mind. Now she says
to take you out for a while."

Amelia Bedelia took Missy
out of the stroller.
"In and out. In and out,"
she said. "I'm plumb tired."

Amelia Bedelia put Missy
in her playpen.
She looked at the list.
"You must be out for good,"
she said.

"It says playtime is
until five o'clock.
Now that is a treat.
I don't get to play much."
Amelia Bedelia looked
around.
"Now what shall I play?"
she said.
She saw Missy's toy box.
"Look at all the toys!"
she said.

Amelia Bedelia sat down.
She began to play.
She played first with one toy.
Then she played with another.
"Oh, what fun!" she said.
"I wish I had toys like these."

Missy began to fuss.
Amelia Bedelia looked
at her watch.
"Shoot!" she said.
"It's five o'clock.
Playtime is over."
She put away the toys.

Then she looked at the list.
"It's time for your supper,"
she said.
"The list says I should
give you some baby food."
Amelia Bedelia picked up Missy.
They went to the kitchen.
Amelia Bedelia put Missy
in her chair.

She took off Missy's sweater
and then read from the list,
"Don't forget
to put on Missy's bib."
Amelia Bedelia found the bib.
"That's plumb cute," she said.
And Amelia Bedelia put it on.

"Now," she said,
"I'll make your supper."
Amelia Bedelia scurried around.
She made baby hamburgers.

She cooked baby potatoes.

She sliced baby tomatoes.

"That is a good supper,"
said Amelia Bedelia.
She started to give it to Missy.
"Oh, oh," she said. "The catsup.
I forgot the catsup."
She poured catsup
over everything.
"Children do love catsup,"
said Amelia Bedelia.
She gave Missy her supper.
Missy tasted it. She smiled.
And Missy ate her supper.

Amelia Bedelia laughed.
"You really liked that," she said.
"You will like this, too."
Amelia Bedelia got a strawberry tart.
"Here," she said.

Missy grabbed the tart.
She ate all of that, too.
"You are a mess,"
said Amelia Bedelia.
"You need washing again."

Mr. and Mrs. Lane came in.

"My baby!" said Mrs. Lane.

"What did you do to her?
What is that red stuff?"

"Red stuff?" said Amelia Bedelia.

"Oh, some of it is catsup,"
she said.
"The rest is strawberries."
"Catsup! Strawberries!"
said Mrs. Lane.
"She can't eat things like that."

"Oh, yes she can,"
said Amelia Bedelia.
"She loves them."
"Why did I leave Missy with you!"
said Mrs. Lane.
"You don't know a thing
about babies."

Mr. Lane ate a strawberry tart.
"Delicious," he said.
"Don't you ever—"
said Mrs. Lane.

But that was as far as she got.
Her mouth was full
of strawberry tart.
"My favorite!" she said.

Missy began to cry.

Mrs. Lane went to her.

But Missy wanted Amelia Bedelia.

"She never did that before,"
said Mr. Lane.

"Amelia Bedelia must know
something we don't."

"I think she knows a lot,"
said Mrs. Lane.

"I'm sorry I got angry.
Will you come again?"

"I would love to,"
said Amelia Bedelia.
"But I have to go now."

Amelia Bedelia walked home.
"I declare," she said.
"That was plumb fun.
Babies are real people.
And I get along
just fine with them."

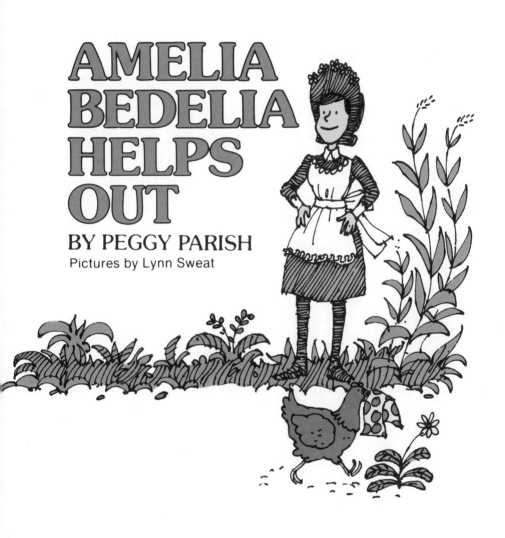

AMELIA BEDELIA HELPS OUT

BY PEGGY PARISH

Pictures by Lynn Sweat

AMELIA BEDELIA HELPS OUT

For Rebecca and Amanda Freedman,
two special young friends,
with love
—P.P.

For Elynor, my wife
—L.S.

"Have a good day,"
said Mr. Rogers.
"And you help your aunt,
Effie Lou."
"I will," said Effie Lou.
"I'll come back for you
late this afternoon,"
said Mr. Rogers.
He drove off.

"What a grand house," said Effie Lou.
"Miss Emma is a grand woman,"
said Amelia Bedelia.
She went to the door and knocked.

"Come in," called Miss Emma.
Amelia Bedelia and Effie Lou
went inside.

"I am glad to see you,"
said Miss Emma.
"Sumter is sick
and my garden is a mess."
"Don't you fret," said Amelia Bedelia.
"We will take care of that.
Just tell us what to do."

"First," said Miss Emma,
"weed the garden."
"All right," said Amelia Bedelia.
"Is there anything else?"
"Yes," said Miss Emma.
"But go ahead
and start
before the sun gets hot."

"Come on, Effie Lou,"
said Amelia Bedelia.
"Let's get busy."
They went to the garden.
"It does have a lot of weeds,"
said Effie Lou.

She started to pull one.

"Stop!" said Amelia Bedelia.

"What are you doing?"

"Trying to get the weeds

out of the garden," said Effie Lou.

"Get them out!" said Amelia Bedelia.
"She said to weed the garden,
not unweed it."
"Oh," said Effie Lou. "I wonder
why she wants more weeds."
Amelia Bedelia thought.

"Those weeds are little," she said.
"Maybe vegetables get hot
just like people. They need
big weeds to shade them.
That's why Miss Emma told us
to weed before the sun gets hot."

"That makes sense," said Effie Lou.

"I see some really big weeds."

"Let's get them," said Amelia Bedelia.

They did.

Soon the garden was weeded.

Amelia Bedelia and Effie Lou
went back to the house.
"The garden is weeded,"
said Amelia Bedelia.

"Good," said Miss Emma.
"Now I want you to stake the beans.
Here is the string to tie them.
You can use this saw
to cut the stakes."
"All right," said Amelia Bedelia.

"There are bugs
on the potato plants.
Take this bug powder
and dust them,"
said Miss Emma.
"If you say so,"
said Amelia Bedelia.

The telephone rang.

Miss Emma went to answer it.

Amelia Bedelia found
all the things she needed.
She and Effie Lou
went back to the garden.

"All right," said Amelia Bedelia.
"We will steak the beans first."
"Have you ever done that?"
said Effie Lou.

"No," said Amelia Bedelia.
"But she just said to steak them.
Anybody can do that."
"Can I help?" said Effie Lou.

"Yes," said Amelia Bedelia.
"You count the bean plants."
Effie Lou counted and said,
"There are fifteen."

Amelia Bedelia
unwrapped the package.
She shook her head and said,
"That's a mighty little bit
of steak for fifteen plants.
But it was all she had."

She took the saw
and cut the steak
into fifteen pieces.

"I could have cut better
with a knife," she said.
"Why didn't you use one?"
said Effie Lou.
"Didn't Miss Emma say to use
this saw?" said Amelia Bedelia.
"Yes," said Effie Lou.

"Then that's why," said Amelia Bedelia.
"Now hold the steak while I tie it."
Amelia Bedelia and Effie Lou
steaked those beans.

"All right, beans,"
said Amelia Bedelia.
"Enjoy your steak."
Effie Lou laughed.

"Your work is fun," she said.
"That it is," said Amelia Bedelia.
"Now those bugs
are waiting to be dusted."
"How do we do that?"
said Effie Lou.

"I'll catch and you dust,"
said Amelia Bedelia.
"Here bug, here buggy, buggy, bug."

They caught and dusted every bug.
"Why did she want us to do that?"
said Effie Lou.
"Most people want bugs killed."
"But Miss Emma is not most people,"
said Amelia Bedelia.
"Those bugs may be her pets.
They are pretty little things."
"If you like bugs,"
said Effie Lou.

"That takes care of that,"
said Amelia Bedelia.
"Let's go in."
"I made lunch for you,"
called Miss Emma.
"After you eat,
throw some scraps
to the chickens."
"All right," said Amelia Bedelia.

"And Amelia Bedelia,"
said Miss Emma, "my garden club
is meeting here this afternoon.
Please make a tea cake."
"I'll be glad to," said Amelia Bedelia.
"I do love to bake."

Amelia Bedelia and Effie Lou
ate their lunch.
"I wonder where she keeps
her scraps?" said Amelia Bedelia.
"I'll ask her."

She went to Miss Emma's room.
She came right back.
"We will have to look for them,"
said Amelia Bedelia.
"She's asleep."

They looked and looked.
"Here's a whole bag of scraps,"
said Effie Lou.
"Good," said Amelia Bedelia.
"Take some and we'll throw them
to the chickens."

They went out to the chicken pen.
Effie Lou threw the scraps.
The chickens came running.
"Look at that!" said Amelia Bedelia.
"I never knew chickens
liked to play."

"Aren't they funny?" said Effie Lou.

"They sure are," said Amelia Bedelia.

"But I've got to get
that tea cake made."

"I never heard of tea cake,"
said Effie Lou.
"Neither have I," said Amelia Bedelia.
"Then how can you make one?"
said Effie Lou.

"Well," said Amelia Bedelia,
"I know what tea is and I know
what cake is. I'll put them together
and I'll have tea cake."
"That's easy," said Effie Lou.

Amelia Bedelia got a mixing bowl.
She put a little of this
and some of that into it.
She mixed and she mixed.
"Now for the tea," she said.

Amelia Bedelia opened some tea bags
and mixed the tea into the batter.
"It looks awful," said Effie Lou.
"Different folks have different tastes,"
said Amelia Bedelia.
She poured the batter into a pan.
Soon the cake was baking.

Amelia Bedelia began to mix
another cake.
"What kind are you making now?"
said Effie Lou.
"Nut cake," said Amelia Bedelia.
"Miss Emma loves that."
Finally the cakes were baked.

"Are you going to put icing
on them?" said Effie Lou.
"That's a good idea,"
said Amelia Bedelia.
"It will fancy them up."
She mixed white icing
and pink icing.

"You ice the tea cake pink," she said.
"I'll ice the nut cake white."

They finished the cakes
and put them away.
Miss Emma came into the kitchen.
"The cake is ready,"
said Amelia Bedelia.
"It smells good," said Miss Emma.

"There's one more thing
I want you to do.
There is a bare spot on my front lawn.
Please sow these grass seeds on it."
"We will be glad to," said Amelia Bedelia.
"Come on, Effie Lou."
They went out front.

"That spot is bare," said Effie Lou.
"It sure is," said Amelia Bedelia.
She sat down and took two needles
and some thread from her bag.
She threaded the needles.
"Here is yours," she said.
"Now, let's sew."

Amelia Bedelia and Effie Lou
sewed those grass seeds
on the bare spot.
"Tie the ends together,"
said Amelia Bedelia.
"We don't want the seed to fall off."

They went into the house.
Miss Emma was in the kitchen.
"Let's walk around some," she said.
"Show me what you've done."
"All right," said Amelia Bedelia.
They walked by the chicken pen.

"Land sakes!" said Miss Emma.

"What are those colored things?"

"Scraps," said Amelia Bedelia.

"Those chickens did have fun."

"My quilting pieces!" said Miss Emma.

"My good quilting pieces!"

"Did we use the wrong scraps?"

said Amelia Bedelia.

"Go get them, Effie Lou."

Miss Emma walked to the garden.
She stopped and stared
"Those weeds!" she said.
"Those big weeds!"

"We got the biggest we could find,"
said Amelia Bedelia.

Miss Emma looked at Amelia Bedelia.
"Thank goodness Sumter
will be back soon," she said.
"Why didn't you stake the beans?"

"We did!" said Amelia Bedelia.
"There just wasn't much steak
to give them.
Show her, Effie Lou."
Effie Lou held up a bush.
"There goes my dinner,"
said Miss Emma.

She looked at the potatoes.
"I see the bugs are dead," she said.
"Dead!" said Amelia Bedelia.
"Did we dust them too much?
I'll get you some more."

Miss Emma laughed and said,
"I can live without them.
You've done enough."
"We enjoyed doing it,"
said Amelia Bedelia.

"I've seen all I want to see,"
said Miss Emma.
They all went inside.
"The ladies should be here soon,"
said Miss Emma.
"The table is set.
The tea is made.
You can put the cake on this tray."
"All right," said Amelia Bedelia.

"I'll let the ladies in,"
said Miss Emma.
She left the kitchen.

"Let's get the cakes ready,"
said Amelia Bedelia.
"I hear the ladies coming now."

Soon Miss Emma called,
"Amelia Bedelia,
please bring the tea."
"Coming," said Amelia Bedelia.
"Bring the cakes, Effie Lou."
Amelia Bedelia set the tea tray
in front of Miss Emma.

"Go ahead and pass the cake,"
said Miss Emma.
Every lady took some cake.
"I'm starved," said Mrs. Lee.
"I can't wait for the tea."
She bit into her cake.

"Delicious!" she said.
"I've never tasted this kind before."
"You've never tasted nut cake?"
said Miss Mary.
"This isn't nut cake," said Mrs. Lee.
"Try the pink kind."

"It is good,"
said Grandma Wilson.
"Hand me another piece."
"There," said Miss Emma,
"your tea is poured."
"Who cares about tea?"
said Mrs. Mark.
"I want more pink cake."

"Emma, do tell us what kind of cake
this is," said Mrs. Bloom.
Miss Emma took some cake.
"My favorite," she said. "Nut cake."
"No, the pink kind," said Ella Jean.
"Try the pink kind."
But all the pink cake was gone.
"Stop keeping secrets,"
said Grandma Wilson.
"What kind of cake was that?"
"Ask Amelia Bedelia,"
said Miss Emma.
"She made it."

A car horn honked outside.

"Mr. Rogers!" said Amelia Bedelia.

"Come on, Effie Lou."

Miss Emma followed
Amelia Bedelia to the kitchen.
"What kind of cake was
the pink one?" she asked.
Amelia Bedelia looked puzzled.
"Tea cake," she said.
"That's what you said to make."
"Tea! You mean—" said Miss Emma.
She began to laugh.

Amelia Bedelia saw something.
"Oh, I plumb forgot," she said.
"Your grass seeds."
Miss Emma looked at them.
She laughed harder
and put them around her neck.

"Amelia Bedelia," she said,
"you are really something.
Effie Lou, you are lucky
to have Amelia Bedelia for an aunt."
"I know," said Effie Lou.
"Amelia Bedelia knows everything."

The horn honked again.
"Hurry, Effie Lou,"
said Amelia Bedelia.
"We can't keep Mr. Rogers waiting."